Jerome   Kima   Lilly   Oli   Sophie   Tom

For Toby - for being such a brave boy
at his new school

Published by Lion Children's Books
an imprint of
Lion Hudson plc
Wilkinson House, Jordan Hill Road,
Oxford OX2 8DR, England
www.lionhudson.com/lionchildrens

Hardback ISBN 978 0 7459 6501 7
Paperback ISBN 978 0 7459 7630 3

First edition 2015

A catalogue record for this book is available from the British Library

Printed and bound in Malaysia, April 2015, LH18

My Stinky New School

Rebecca Elliott

LION
CHILDREN'S

Clemmie goes to a special school.

It smells of rainbows,

paint,

and chocolate,

and she loves it.

Benjamin goes to nursery.

It smells of **sunshine**,
playdough,
and **bananas**,

and he loves it.

Today I start at my new school.

It stinks of pigeon poop,
ogre **armpits**,
and **sadness**.

And I hate it.

I have no friends.

And I don't know my way around.

I'm like a lonely lost **spaceman**.

Luckily there is an alien called **Jake**
who says he'll help me.

He tells me where you hang your spacesuit,

Isaac   Bernard   Toby   Amira   ake   Ali

where you eat your
moon cheese sandwich,

and where to go if you
need an astro poop.

"But where do I find new friends?" I wonder.

Then Jake shows me the playground
where there's a massive pirate ship.

I meet a pirate called Lilly
and we sail the seven seas for a bit.

We land on an island,
find buried treasure,
and meet some **mermaids**.

No new friends though.

Back in the classroom Mrs Appleton talks to us about dinosaurs.

A chap called Bernard tells me he's an expert.

We go on a dinosaur hunt
together and find three
velociraptors,

a T-rex, and a brachiosaurus.

But no friendosaurus.

When Mum comes to pick me up, she asks how my day's been.

"Fine," I say. "I met an alien, sailed the seven seas, and hunted a velociraptor."

"OK," says Mum. "And did you make any friends?"

"No," I say sadly.

"Well who are all those people then?" says Mum.

My new school DOES stink.
It stinks of moon cheese,
buried treasure, and dinosaurs.

And I LOVE it.